Baby Brown Bear's
Big Bellyache

By Eugene Bradley Coco
Illustrated by John Nez

A GOLDEN BOOK • NEW YORK
Western Publishing Company, Inc., Racine, Wisconsin 53404

© 1989 Western Publishing Company, Inc. All rights reserved. Printed in the U.S.A. No part of this book may be reproduced or copied in any form without written permission from the publisher. All trademarks are the property of Western Publishing Company, Inc. Library of Congress Catalog Card Number: 88-51412 ISBN: 0-307-12088-0/ ISBN: 0-307-62088-3 (lib. bdg.) A B C D E F G H I J K L M

There is a magical place called Little Golden Book Land, filled with wonderful things to see and do. Every day is a special day, just waiting to be discovered.

Baby Brown Bear was in a hurry. Today was the day of the Little Golden Book Land Picnic, and he didn't want to be late. As fast as he could, Baby Brown Bear made his bed, brushed his teeth, and did his chores. Then he went downstairs for breakfast.

His mother gave him a big bowlful of cereal topped with a spoonful of honey.

"Be sure and eat all of your cereal," she said. "It should fill you up until lunchtime."

When he was finished, Baby Brown Bear's mother went over to the cupboard and took down a big jar of honey for Baby Brown Bear to take to the picnic. "This should be enough for everyone," she told Baby Brown Bear as she put the jar in a knapsack and handed it to her son.

"Now, promise," she added, "that you won't eat all the honey on the way. You know that too much honey makes you feel sick."

"I promise," said Baby Brown Bear. He slung the knapsack over his shoulder and went out the door.

With a smile on his face, Baby Brown Bear set
off for Hilly Meadows, the wide, open field where
the big picnic was to be held.

Baby Brown Bear hadn't traveled very far when
he felt a rumble in his stomach. "A little bit of
honey will quiet that," he thought. He quickly
forgot about his promise and took a handful of
honey from the honey jar.

A short while later he felt a tumble in his stomach. "I'll have just a bit more honey from the honey jar," said Baby Brown Bear.

A little while after THAT he felt a RUMBLE and a TUMBLE in his stomach, so he ate even MORE of the honey from the honey jar!

By the time Baby Brown Bear got to the picnic, there was only a drop of honey left in the honey jar, and he had the biggest bellyache ever.

"Maybe I should have listened to my mother," thought Baby Brown Bear.

"Come roll with us," said Shy Little Kitten and Poky Little Puppy.

"I don't think so," Baby Brown Bear replied. "I have a bellyache."

"Rolling makes you forget about everything," said Poky Little Puppy. "I'm sure it will make your bellyache go away."

So Baby Brown Bear joined his two little friends, but after a few minutes his belly began to ache even more.

"What's the matter?" asked Saggy Baggy
Elephant.

"I ate all the honey in the honey jar," moaned
Baby Brown Bear. "Now my belly aches."

"Well, every time I have a bellyache," said Saggy
Baggy Elephant, "I just dance and it disappears."

So Baby Brown Bear joined Saggy and their
friends, and together they danced–one-two-three-
kick! One-two-three-kick!–but that didn't help
much, either.

"The best thing for a bellyache is carrot stew," said Tawny Scrawny Lion as he set a fresh bowl of it in front of Baby Brown Bear.

Baby Brown Bear had never cared much for carrot stew, but knowing that Tawny Scrawny Lion always gave good advice, he decided to try some.

Baby Brown Bear ate the carrot stew...and he ate it...and he ate it...and he ate it...until all of it was gone. And that was more than his stomach could take.

"What am I going to do now?" moaned Baby Brown Bear.

"Come for a swim," called Scuffy, who was floating around in the nearby stream.

"Maybe the water will help," whimpered Baby Brown Bear as he joined Scuffy.

However, whenever he or Scuffy moved, the water wiggled, and then the wiggles turned into waves, and before he knew it, Baby Brown Bear's face was turning all sorts of colors and his belly was going *swish-swosh...swish-swosh...swish-swosh!*

"That didn't help at all," Baby Brown Bear said
sadly when he was back on shore. "If only I were
home. My mother would sing me a lullaby and rub
my belly. Then the ache would surely go away."

"Well, what are we waiting for!" said Tootle.
"Next stop, Cavetown!"

Baby Brown Bear raced into his mother's arms. "I broke my promise and I ate all the honey from the honey jar on the way to the picnic. Now I'm sorry I did it, and I'm sorry I broke my promise, and I have the biggest bellyache ever," he sobbed.

"There, there," soothed his mother. "Mama's here." Then she lifted Baby Brown Bear onto her lap and very gently began to rub his stomach. She softly sang a sweet lullaby.

By the next day, Baby Brown Bear's big bellyache was long gone. But he now knew that a promise was a promise and had to be kept and that he was certainly never going to eat an entire jar of honey again.

At least not all at once!